BLUE JAY GIRL

and

LION SINGER

Illustrations in Black and White

BLUE JAY GIRL

and

LION SINGER

Two Stories for Children

by

Sylvia Ross

Black and White Illustrations Edition
~~<<<>>>~~
Bentley Avenue Books

BLUE JAY GIRL AND LION SINGER, TWO STORIES FOR CHILDREN

ISBN: 978-0-578-46272-1
COPYRIGHT: Sylvia Ross

***For parents and teachers: There are many empty pages in this book. This space intentionally provides a place for children to draw or write in the book, one of the joys of ownership of a print book. ***

Table of Contents

BLUE JAY GIRL

by

Sylvia Ross

This compiled second edition of the two books is dedicated to the children of the Tule River Indian Reservation, and also to the author and her husband's great grandchildren as of 2019: Houston and Hadley Webber; Nixon, Pace, and Dash Thompkins; Lydia, Roberto, and Frida Ochoa; and Eleanor and Birdie Powell. And, to any more that may come in the future.

BLUE JAY GIRL

PRONUNCIATION GUIDE

It is common in the dialect of the Yokuts tribes of California's languages, which include both the Yaudanchi and the Chukchansi, that every vowel is given a syllable of its own. Capitalized words are the names of tribes or places.

ahntru (ahn tru)
Apiche (A pi che)
chineu (chin e oo)
Choiumne (Choi um ne)
Chukchansi (Chuk chan si)
Dumna (Dum na)
homud (ho mud)
kahuhpe (kah uh pe)
kiyu   (ki yu)
kouteun (kou te un)
Koyeti (Koy et i)
idik (id ik)
Monache (Mon a chi)
mukec (mu kec)
opodo (o po do)
Pawhawuh Tin (paw haw uh Tin)
Tachi (Ta chi)
trahushnah (trah ush nah)
trahud (trah ud)
tripne (trip ni)
Tulumne (Tu lum ni)
Wakchumne (Wak chum ni)
Yaudanche (Yau dan chi)
Yowlumne (Yow lum ni)

Yaet > One

~~~<oOo>~~~

Once, on the rim of a great valley, just where the hills turned into mountains, there lived a medium sized Yaudanchi girl. She'd been named for a blue jay who had flown by her house right after she was born. She lived in her tribe's village, which was called Pawhawwuh Tin. It was near a river that wound down to the valley from the high mountains.

Now the mountains are called the Sierra Nevada, the valley is called the San Joaquin and the river is called the Tule; but in those days long ago, everything had different names.

Blue Jay Girl looked like any girl in the tribe. She had dark hair and tan skin. When she smiled her eyes sparkled, and she had deep dimples in her cheeks. She smiled often.

To look at her, you wouldn't think that she was dangerous, and the people of the tribe seemed to like her. She was respectful to all the people in her village. She had a soft voice and never yelled at anyone. Well, if all the children were racing through the oak trees, she would sometimes yell to her friends, but never in a mean way. She never yelled in the village where she might wake babies or annoy elders.

To look at Blue Jay Girl you would think she was an ordinary girl. But she was not ordinary. She was a girl who went where she wanted to go. She did what she wanted to do. She was afraid of nothing. Although she always worked hard to do what she was supposed to do to help her family, when she was finished she didn't sit and play quiet games. She went to find adventures.

When the other girls were learning to make baskets, Blue Jay Girl ran to follow trails in the woods. She climbed trees and explored caves, and played in the oak woods.

When the other girls were helping their mothers and aunties shell acorns, Blue Jay Girl was hiding in the rocks spying on the boys. When the other girls were down at the river learning women's washing songs, Blue Jay Girl was dancing in the meadow making up her own songs.

Still, when the other girls of the tribe wanted to play, they ran to find Blue Jay Girl. They wanted to be with her. The girls all knew that a girl who *wasn't* ordinary was much more fun than a girl who was ordinary.

Poonoy >> Two

It was the time of a year when flowers were blooming. The sun was bright and there were birds flying all around because the cold clouds of winter were gone.

Blue Jay Girl had a good family who loved her, and a little dog of her own. He was called Kiyu. Until now, her life had always pleased her and she had been happy.

Today she was the very saddest girl in the village.

She walked away from the village houses and Kiyu followed her. She walked along the trail to the bathing place at the river. As the river trail went down a rocky slope, Blue Jay Girl stubbed her toe. It didn't bleed, but it hurt. It was a little thing, but it made her even more unhappy. As she walked on toward the river, her throat got dry. Though she tried to swallow down her tears, sadness filled her.

She remembered what her mother had said that morning while they worked together. She had been helping her mother put out strips of bear meat to dry, and her mother noticed that she was very quiet.

"Where is your voice today, little one?" her mother asked.

Blue Jay Girl didn't want to answer. but it would be rude not to answer an older person, especially when the older person was one's mother.

"My voice doesn't want to come out of me," she said.

Her mother handed her the basket of dry herbs to rub into the fresh meat. "What is making your voice so shy? Then her mother said, "Usually you have lots of funny stories to tell me when we work."

The girl answered slowly. "I haven't any funny stories. I'm not happy and everything makes me sad."

"Tell me why you are sad," her mother said. "I like you better when you are happy."

Blue Jay Girl thought for a minute as she worked. She rubbed the herbs into the meat and the herbs smelled good and spicy. Then she answered her mother. "I'm sad because my friends don't want to be with me. I'm sad because not even Fierce Badger will come to play with me. The girls all run away if I go where they are. I know they still like me. But they won't play with me."

"No. They can't play with you," Her mother quietly said. She knelt down on the ground and began to stack more pieces of meat to hang. "Their families don't want them to be with you."

"Why don't they?" Blue Jay Girl asked. "I don't say or do mean things,"

"It's because you are too dangerous." Blue Jay Girl mother said as she kept working. She didn't look at her daughter.

"I'm not dangerous!" the little girl said. She didn't look at her mother either.

"Yes, you are," her mother answered, never looking up.

They finished their work without talking to each other.

~~~<oOo>~~~

Souhpun <<< Three

After the work was finished, Blue Jay Girl decided to go on a walk away from her home. Lupine flowers and poppies were blooming along their path. Kiyu jumped in the flowers, but she wouldn't pay attention to him. She didn't notice the blue and orange flowers.

They walked until they came to the bathing part of the river. No one else was around and they both jumped in the water. It was swift and shivery cold, because the river was flowing down from melting snow on the high mountains.

Blue Jay Girl scrubbed beneath her finger nails and washed her hair with soap plant. She swam a little while and got out in the sun to dry. She twirled around so her skirt could dry too. Kiyu shook himself. Water sprayed all around them. Today, it didn't make her laugh.

They sat down on the sandy river bank so the sun could warm them. The dog went to sleep in a hollow he made in the sand. Blue Jay Girl was thinking and thinking. A breeze came and made the river weeds tremble. Kiyu flicked his ear. Blue Jay Girl remembered what her mother had said.

I'm not dangerous, she thought, looking into the clear water in the river.

But then, she imagined how her mother's calm face would change if she had seen Blue Jay Girl jump into the river. She knew her mother would think it was a dangerous thing to do when no other people were around. Blue Jay Girl got up and began walking. Kiyu made circles around her as they walked on through the low hills.

Suddenly, a blue jay came darting down from the sky. The blue jay almost collided with them then changed direction so quickly they couldn't see where he went. The bird called "Cay Cay" from one of the trees as though he were teasing her. As sad as she was, Blue Jay Girl laughed at the blue jay. She liked those noisy birds.

They continued on to the place where there were rocks under three big oak trees. *I know I'm not dangerous*, she thought. She'd been born in the time of ripe acorns and everyone knew that ripe acorn children were lucky.

She'd had the usual little accidents all children have, but she'd never really gotten hurt. She'd never even been sick.

I'm lucky, she thought. *I'm too lucky to be dangerous.*

~~~~~~

Hoppoonoy <<<< Four

Instead of being sad, Blue Jay Girl began to get angry. She stamped her foot. She sat down hard on a big rock. There was no reason for her friends to abandon her.

She was the least dangerous person she had ever known. She had never even hurt herself any worse than a skinned knee or a sore toe.

On the ground by her feet she saw some stones. She grimaced, and then she picked a stone up and looked back toward the village. It was far away, behind them, down the trail.

She frowned. The village was not nice to her. No one was nice to her. People thought she was dangerous and she wasn't. Kiyu stared up at her and wagged his tail, but she ignored him.

She flipped the stone in her hand up and down.

Then she stood up and stretched as tall as she could. She aimed the stone at the village. But as she threw it, the stone flew out of her hand wrong. It went the opposite direction. It went spinning up into the trees and made blue jays come swooping out. Then plop! The stone came down, and it nearly hit Kiyu's head.

Blue Jay Girl looked down at her little dog. She had almost caused him to get hurt. She startled the jays that she had been named for. She couldn't even throw a stone right anymore.

If her brother had been here, she thought, he would have laughed at her.

Three blue feathers came fluttering down from the tree. One landed on the rock where she sat. The other two landed near on the ground near Kiyu. She picked the feathers up and put them in the pouch where she kept her year stones.

It had been a bad day. But, blue feathers were good for a Blue Jay Girl. She was lucky.

She felt a little better, as she sat there under the trees with Kiyu leaning against her legs.

But then, she began to remember things that had happened. She realized why people thought she was dangerous. While she wasn't dangerous to herself, she was dangerous to others.

No, she thought. *Those things happened when I was little. They weren't my fault.*

~~~~~~

Yachcheenil <<<<< Five

Blue Jay Girl then remembered how when she was very small, she had once nearly walked into danger.

Her father and her brother had trapped a raccoon. It was fuzzy and its fur looked soft. She wanted to hug it, like she hugged her mother's puppies.

Barely in time, her brother pushed her out of the way of the raccoon's teeth, but the sharp teeth tore the skin on brother's leg and he still had a scar.

She remembered that when she had only six acorn seasons, she had been chasing some dragonflies and had fallen into a deep, fast part of the river. Her mother's sister almost drowned trying to save her. Auntie had jumped in and pushed Blue Jay Girl to the shallows of the river and to safety, but before Auntie could get out herself, the fast current carried her downstream.

Men who were fishing far down the river saved Auntie, but she choked up much water before she could breathe again.

Blue Jay Girl knew why the people of the village might *think* she was dangerous. But she knew she wasn't. Those were just accidents.

Blue Jay Girl, with Kiyu following her, left the trees and soon found themselves near Kahunpe Meadow. She heard girls laughing, and she and Kiku went to see what the girls were doing. Blue Jay Girl's best friends were there. They were sitting in the meadow flowers, using blue blossoms to squeeze purple-blue juice out.

Fierce Badger, Reaches Too Far, Small Ants Crawling, and Fierce Badger's little sister Blue Crow were rubbing the juice on their faces to make tattoos like their mothers wore. Fierce Badger had three lines of flower juice on her chin. So did the other girls.

That was fun and it made Blue Jay Girl smile. The girls greeted her and called her. She knew they were happy to see her. But she just waved and turned away from them.

If she joined them, they would have to break up their play. One by one, each of her friends would go home. Their mothers didn't want them to be with her. So, she couldn't stay and ruin their fun, even if they asked her to.

It wouldn't be fair.

~~~~~~

Chulapee <<<<< **Six**

Blue Jay Girl turned away and walked back to the place of the oak trees. She thought about the girls putting tattoos on their faces and arms. As she thought about her friends she remembered the very worst thing that had ever happened in her life. She knew that her mother and the village people were right.

The worst thing had happened before the last acorn season, in the season when the sun was hot and grass turned yellow.

She had nine quartz stones in the pouch to mark her years. She knew she would get a tenth stone when acorn season came. She began exploring and found something fun to do.

She climbed up on a craggy rock and boosted herself up until she could pull herself into a big tree. From the tree, she could watch the boys play hoop games and race each other. The boys couldn't see her and that made it more fun. They couldn't chase her away if they didn't see her.

Her friends began giggling but the wind was good to them and the boys didn't hear. The girls began to climb into the tree. Fierce Badger climbed up first and found a branch for herself and her sister.

Blue Crow helped Reaches Too Far up into the tree. The tree began to fill up with girls giggling and whispering. Small Ants Crawling climbed up last. She couldn't find a place to sit. Blue Jay Girl moved farther out on her branch so there was room for her friend.

The girls didn't realize that the branch had rotted out underneath. It broke with a loud creaking sound, and then a snap, and the two girls came crashing down.

Blue Jay Girl landed in old leaves and soft dirt. But Small Ants Crawling fell onto the rock that the girls had used to boost themselves into the tree.

Small Ants Crawling was badly hurt. Her arm was broken. She grew very sick. Her family had to call the frightening Opodo Kouteun to come and sing for her. The girls stood far back because they were all afraid of the tripne man.

Opodo's wife Idik Mukec, the tribe's healer woman, came too. She limped along behind him as fast as she could, carrying her healer's basket. She sang quietly with her husband while she washed Small Ants Crawling's arm and bound it up in moss and willow branches.

Idik Mukec came to see Small Ants Crawling every day, bringing medicine until the sickness and fever were finally gone. The girl's arm finally healed, but it was scarred and crooked.

Opodo Kouteun went to the tribe's sweat house and he made the men all sing with him and do healing dances for Small Ants Crawling. But it didn't look like her arm would straighten out again.

Idik Mukec taught Small Ants Crawling how to strap her arm across her body so it didn't hurt too much. She brought a band of rattlesnake rattles for the child to wear on her arm so it would grow strong again. Everyone knew that *trahud*, rattlesnake, had a powerful spirit.

I am dangerous. Blue Jay Girl thought. *I can't have friends anymore because people don't want their children hurt.*

She and Kiyu turned to follow the trail back to the village. Blue Jay Girl knew she would be lonely forever. She was just too dangerous to have friends.

~~~~~~

Numchen <<<<< << Seven

Blue Jay Girl went back home. On the way, she met her brother who gave her a feather from a woodpecker and a striped feather with a red quill from the flicker bird. But her brother didn't have time to talk with her. Brother was on his way to get honey from a bee tree.

When she reached home, she gave her mother the feathers her brother had given her.

"Ah, these are fine feathers. I will thank brother." Her mother said. "I especially like feathers from flicker bird. Many of flicker's quills are yellow. Red ones like this are hard to find."

"The Blue Jays gave me feathers today," Blue Jay Girl told her mother.

She put her arms around her mother and hugged her. She decided to ask her mother a very serious question.

"Mother, how can I change my nature?" she asked.

The woman thought before she answered. Then she said, "Maybe you can't change your nature, Little One. I think your nature is bold like the blue jay, not careful like the quail."

"I want to be a quail. Little quail birds always take good care of each other."

Her mother smiled a wistful smile. "I would tell you how to change your nature if I could. Mother quail is not bold or as beautiful as the sky, but she does take good care of her babies."

They sat together for a long time. Blue Jay Girl's mother made a necklace for her daughter with the three blue jay feathers, some dried red and black berries and pitch from the pine trees. She strung them on a length of cord Blue Jay Girl's father had made by twisting the strings from long weeds.

She put the feather necklace around Blue Jay Girl neck and said, "You are a beautiful child.

~~~~~~

Moonosh <<<<< <<< **Eight**

Blue Jay Girl's mother had said she was a beautiful child, and she felt like one. But Blue Jay Girl had something important to do.

Sometimes a girl has to do things for herself, so she told Kiyu to stay home. She went back down to the river alone. She walked along the riverbank.

She walked past the drinking place, then the place where her father caught silvery fish in nets, and then the place where people bathed and swam. Soon, she passed the place where the women cleaned skins and furs and the place where men bathed and had their sweat house.

Blue Jay Girl had walked the length of the village along the river. She saw she had come to the last house. She was standing at the narrow path to Opodo Kouteun's house. It was a spooky, frightening place. None of the children she knew had ever gone near the tripne man's home.

The tribe's chief lived at one end of the village. He guarded the village from bears, wolves and lions. Opodo Kouteun lived at the other end. He guarded the village from ghosts, bad spirits and evil things. The tripne man could see into the spirits of all the animals. Everyone said he could see into people's spirits too.

Blue Jay Girl didn't think she wanted to go where someone might see into her spirit.

The little girl knew that Idik Mukec, the ahntru woman, lived there with Opodo Kouteun. The healer woman was always kind. But knowing that Idik Mukek was kind didn't give Blue Jay Girl courage. She wanted to turn around and run home.

Instead her feet walked her straight to Opodo Kouteun's house.

Long sharp bear claws, with wolf and bear skulls, were propped on the shrubs and hanging all around the area. There was a lion skin hanging from the chineu near the house.

Blue Jay Girl had seen dead animals all her life. She knew the lion skin wouldn't hurt her. But it looked like it would. Its head was hanging down. Someone had made eyes for it of pitch and shell pieces. They glittered in the sun. The lion looked alive, and as though he were waiting to pounce.

She was glad she had left Kiyu at home. He'd be more afraid of the lion skin than she was.

~~~~~~

Sopunhut <<<<< <<<< **Chapter Nine**

As she came along the path, Blue Jay Girl knew that she should have brought presents to give the tripne and ahntru elders. She was sorry she didn't have anything to give them.

Idik Mukec was sitting on the ground grinding acorn meal. The old woman looked up and pointed at Blue Jay Girl. "I know who you are," Idik Mukec said. "You are the bold girl." She chuckled as she said it, as though being bold was good.

Most of the people in the village didn't think bold was a good thing to be. But, Idik Mukec wasn't like ordinary people. She was a healer, an ahntru woman. The girl thought of a gift. She took the necklace her mother had made for her and gave it to the old woman. Idik Mukec admired its three blue feathers, and put it around her own neck.

Just then Opodo Keutoun came roaring out of the house. "Who is this person?" he asked in a gruff, loud voice. He had a mask on his head and wore a band of vulture feathers on his shoulders.

Blue Jay Girl's knees were shaking. Her hands were shaking as she offered the pouch to the tripne man. Opodo Keutoun opened it and counted out the nine white quartz stones.

Making her voice brave, the little girl said, "I am Blue Jay Girl. I have nine acorn seasons. I came to ask if you could help me change my nature. I don't want to be dangerous anymore."

The old man scrunched up his face and frowned, "Everything is what it is," he said. "Rabbit runs on the ground and fish swims in the river. Rabbit doesn't swim and fish doesn't run." He turned away from her.

"I know," she answered, not rudely but in her strongest voice. "But blue jay and quail are both birds. They fly and build nests. In much they are the same."

Opodo Keutoun looked at her. She was afraid he was angry. Maybe he would send her away. "Couldn't blue jay learn to be like a quail?" She softly asked.

Instead of being looking angry, the tripne man's mouth curled up in a smile. He slowly sat down on the ground beside his wife.

Then he looked up at Blue Jay Girl and said, "Let me sing. I will sing and find an answer to the question of birds and natures."

Treeo <<<<< <<<<< **Chapter Ten**

Opodo Kouteun shook the nine acorns in the pouch, and began to sing. Idik Mukec began to sing too. She sang a different song than her husband was singing, for she was an ahntru woman, not a tripne man. Their voices blended together.

Blue Jay Girl had never heard a two-voice song as beautiful. Her heart beat slower and she began to feel calm.

Her sadness disappeared as the voices floated in the air around her, gruff and sweet.

Opodo Keutoun and Idik Mukec stopped singing and smiled at each other. The sun had moved. It was soft on their faces.

The tripne man said, "You are a dangerous girl. It is hard to change one's nature. But, I believe I know a way."

He began to talk to her. "You must teach yourself to move slowly and think carefully," he said. "Birds can dart away from trouble because they are quick. They have wings as well as legs.

"Birds use both the earth and the sky. The Yaudanchi people have legs, but no wings. It is hard for people to escape danger.

We must be more careful. Will you teach yourself to look ahead and recognize what would be dangerous for the Yaudanchi people?"

"I will," she answered again.

"That is not all. There is more you must do. Until two acorn seasons have passed, you must come here every day. You must help my wife go to the washing place at the river because it is hard for her to walk so far now that she is old. I help her with her work but I can't take her to the women's place.

"And, there is more. You must learn the ahntru medicines. You will have to learn the names of plants and where to find them. This work will help you to be careful."

"I'll come every day," she answered.

Treeo yaet <<<<< <<<<< < **Chapter Eleven**

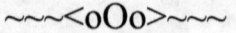

Blue Jay Girl went home. She asked her parents if she could go to the tripne man's house every morning to help Idik Mukec. They agreed and seemed to be proud of her.

Her brother was amazed. Even the big boys stayed away from Opodo Kouteun's house with its skulls and skins and totems.

"You're brave, little sister," Blue Jay Girl's brother told her.

The next morning, when family work was done, Blue Jay Girl went down the trail to begin changing her nature.

This day nothing frightened her. The skulls were just skulls. The lion just looked like an old skin. Without the mask, Opodo Kouteun looked like her grandfather. He wasn't even a little scary. He gave her back the pouch that held her nine - year stones.

Blue Jay Girl helped Idik Mukec go down to the river. Blue Jay Girl had to walk very slowly. The girl helped the old woman get down into the bathing pool of the washing place and found soap plant for her. She helped her wash her hair. Then, slowly and carefully, she helped the old woman back to her house.

The tripne man was pleased when his wife told him how Blue Jay Girl had helped her.

"You did good work", the tripne man said to the little girl.

"Now Idik Mukec can teach you about plants and about healing. She will teach you something new every day. But you must learn. Can you do that?

Blue Jay Girl remembered all the days she had seen Idik Mukec come to help people throughout the village. Idik Mukec helped everyone who needed her.

"Yes. I can." She said. "I don't like weaving baskets, but I want to learn what Idik Mukec can teach me. When I learn the medicine teas, I will know where to find them," the little girl said, for she remembered the plants that grew in all the places she had explored. "I want to learn to help people."

The Tripne man's wife turned to Blue Jay Girl. She looked very serious. "You must keep blue jay's spirit, little girl," she said.

"Why must I?" Blue Jay asked. "I want to have quail's spirit."

"Healers must be as careful as little quail, but healers must also be as bold as the blue jays. Healers face hard tasks. They must be brave as well as tender."

The old woman took off the necklace with three blue feathers. She put it back on Blue Jay Girl. "Keep your own spirit. It is a good one. Call to quail's spirit when you need it."

Then Idik Mukec looked at her husband. She said, "I knew that a dangerous girl might be just what we needed to help us." The old people looked at each. Then they smiled at Blue Jay Girl.

Opodo Kouteun bent down and told her, "It will take a long time for the Yaudanchi people to see that your nature has changed. You must be patient. Your friends will not come back soon. It will be hard for you to wait."

Blue Jay Girl knew it would be hard, but she knew she could do it.

Treeo poonoy <<<<< <<<<< << **Twelve**

Blue Jay Girl was right. She could do it. She did do it. Long before one acorn season had passed, she had all her friends back. Their parents could see that their children would be safe with her.

Her friends helped her find, gather and dry medicine plants. The girls still climbed trees to spy on boys, but they checked to make sure all the branches were sturdy enough to hold them.

*

Before Blue Jay Girl had lived for *thirty* acorn seasons, she was known as the greatest ahntru woman of the whole Yokuts nation. She was the Blue Jay Woman.

She went from village to village, tribe to tribe, to where ever anyone needed her. She treated people's wounds and had medicines for their sicknesses. She went as far as she needed to go, and she was never afraid.

Blue Jay Woman traveled far beyond the tribes of the Koyeti, the Yowlumni, the Choiumni, and the Wakchumni.

She climbed the great mountains to the east. She went to the cool country of the north. She went to the deserts of the south. And, she went to the west until she came to the great ocean.

Wherever she went, she helped people. However far she traveled, she always returned to Pawhawwuh Tin. She brought back new medicine plants and remedies she had learned for her own Yaudanchi people.

Blue Jay Girl had kept her own nature and she gained another. For all her long life, she carried two spirits with her, the spirit of trahushnah, the blue jay, and the spirit of homud, the quail.

~~~<oOo>~~~

A Vocabulary of Yaudanchi Words Used in This Book:

ahntru = a healer, a doctor for the body. A Chukchansi woman could become an ahntru.

chineu = a pole shelter

homud = quail

kahuhpe = water grass

kiyu = coyote

kouteun = a priest, a healer for the spirit or soul. A woman could not become a kouteun.

idik = water

mukec = woman

trahud = rattlesnake

opodo = the sun

Pawhawwuh Tin = Blue Jay Girl's village

tripne = the spirit world

trahushnah = blue jay

****

LION SINGER

by

Sylvia Ross

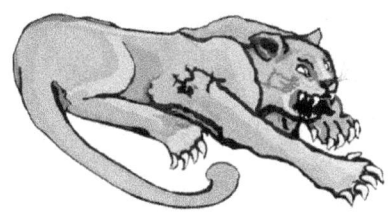

PRONUNCIATION GUIDE

Notes: It is common in the Chukchansi dialect of the Yokuts language that every vowel is sounded.

Tsuloniu (Tsu-lo-nee-oo)

Suksanau (Suk-sa-na-oo)

Apasau or Hapasau (Ah–pah-sah-oo)

Kataniu (Ka-ta-nee-oo)

LION SINGER

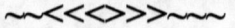

Chapter One

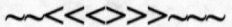

There was once a time when there was no metal in the Chukchansi people's world. There was no metal, so there were no clocks or frying pans. There were no barbecue grills. There were no electronics. There were no cars or trucks. There were no wristwatches or computers or television sets. There were no cell phones.

There was not one single nail in the land of the Chukchansi. Even if there had been metals to make soda cans, no one had invented soda. The Chukchansi drank cool water from rivers and streams when they were thirsty.

Of course, back then, there were no white people on this side of the mountains. There were no black people either. The mountains to the east were so high that buffalo and horses had never crossed them to come to the hill country of the Chukchansi.

Far to the west, across California's great valley, stories were told of strange pale people who came and brought odd animals to the Ohlone people of the coastal lands.

But swamps covered the valley between the Chukchansi people and the Ohlone people, so those strange people with their strange animals had never come to the Chukchansi village of Tsuloniu, Kataniu, Apasau, and Chikchanan.

In the land of the Chukchansi there were no cows, bur there wee deer, antelope, and mountain sheep. There were no chickens, but there were quail, blue jays, hawks and eagles.

The Chukchansi shared all these good things of the earth with their neighbors to the north, the Miwok, and their cousins, the other Yokuts to the south.

It was a good place to live.

~~~~~~

Chapter Two

The **Chukchansi people had** four big villages: Tsuloniu, Kataniu, Apasau, and Chikchanan. Three or four times a year, the members of the tribe got together and had a campout. Sometimes the campout would be in one village, and sometimes it would be in another.

When the villages got together, the children could run free. The adults in their families were busy planning songs and dances, telling stories, and making food.

Sometimes when the adults were busy, the children got into trouble. But usually they were good and there were no troubles.

Chukchansi teenagers were supposed to watch the medium-sized children. Medium-sized children were supposed to watch the little children. No one had to watch the Chukchansi babies, because they were in cradleboards and their mothers took care of them.

One summer, there was a big camp-out in the village of Apasau. All the villages would gather there.

Dog Cry was a medium-sized boy. He came from the village of Kataniu. It was the village of his mother's clan lived.

It was the custom among the Chukchansi, that fathers would live with their wives and children in the village of their wives' families.

Dog Cry was happy to be at the summer camp-out because he could run and play with his cousins who lived in his father's village. His cousins knew all the secret places around the village. They knew places where children could go and no one would bother them.

~~~~~~~~~~~~~~~~~~~~~~~~~~~~~~~~~~~~~~

Chapter Three

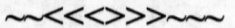

Dog Cry was expected to watch his little sister while all the grownups were busy setting up camp. His parents had much to do and were busy.

He knew that was his responsibility. He didn't have any other sisters or brothers who could watch out for her. His mother had to work at preparing food. His father had to help set up poles to make shade over the area where food would be served.

But his cousins called to him, and he decided to play with them in the oak woods beyond the camp.

His little sister, who was called Breaks Shells, began to follow him. Dog Cry wanted to be with his cousins, not with a wee little girl, so he took her hand and led her back to the camp to the place where the elders sat in the shade.

He thought that that the elders would watch over her. Everyone liked Breaks Shells, for she laughed a lot. And the elders didn't have to do anything else for they were old.

He could leave her with them, and he could go and play with his cousins. It was a good plan.

When Breaks Shells saw her great-grandmother, she ran on her fat little legs and jumped into the old woman's lap. Great-grandmother smiled and cuddled her.

Dog Cry was free!

He quickly turned and ran away before Great-grandmother could call him back.

~~~~~~

Chapter Four

Dog Cry's cousins were waiting for him on the path in the meadow behind the elder's shelter. They were acting rowdy and silly.

They told him about a special place at the top of a hill. The hill was rocky and rose up at the far end of the campground. It was taller than the other hills around the meadow.

The boys followed the meadow path. It led past some thick berry bushes.

Behind the berry bushes there was a gully where winter rains sometimes made a creek. In the summer it was wide and dry, and the boys tried to jump across. On the other side, the cousins began to climb the hill that rose just beyond the gully's edge.

They climbed until they came to a place where rocks had long ago come down and made a big sloping pile on the steep hillside. Cousin Flea broke a short branch from a small oak tree and the other boys did the same. The boys knew to scrape the branches on the rocks in front of them as they climbed across the rock fall.

Nassis, the name that people called the rattlesnake, lived in the rocks. The cousins wanted to warn Nassis that they were climbing through his land.

Even though the snake was a creature of great power, he was very shy. When he heard the branches scraping he would slip away.

The boys' mothers had taught them this when they were very small. No Chukchansi woman would cross through rocks or go off a path without branch in her hand scrape on the ground to warn Nassis. It was polite to warn Nassis if you were coming to a place where he lived.

Cousins were the very best thing in Dog Cry's life, because he had no brothers. His father's older wife had three girls, and his mother, the younger wife, had only Dog Cry and his little sister. In his home village of Kataniu, Dog Cry had many friends, but they were not the same as cousins.

The boys scrambled up and over the rock pile and found themselves high on a ledge overlooking the whole campground.

Far down below them, Dog Cry and his cousins could see their fathers with the men from all the Chukchansi villages.. The men were building shelters, fishing, and clearing a place for the singing and dancing later that evening.

The boys could see their mothers and the women building a long cooking fire, and they could hear the laughing of the women in the camp. He could see the elders sitting in the shade of the shelter. He saw Great-grandmother, but he didn't see his sister.

One of his cousins called to him. The boys were laughing again as they raced each other in climbing up the ledge to get to the top of the hill.

The oldest of his cousins was a quiet, tall boy who was called Always Angry. He seldom spoke and almost never smiled, but the boys all liked him. Always Angry grabbed a knotty little tree and pulled himself up and climbed until he was two man lengths above the other boys.

Dog Cry wanted to climb with his cousins, but he was worried. He didn't see his sister with the elders. He didn't know where she was.

He looked at the elders as they sat talking. He still could not see his sister. He could see where the women of the four villages were preparing food. He could see his mother lift her cooking basket and go toward the fire line.

Little Breaks Shells was not with her.

Looking down at the camp, he could see the narrow path where he had run to meet his cousins. It ran from the campground across the meadow to the bottom of the hill. He saw the dry meadow grass all yellow in the sun.

Far from the elders, far from the campground, and deep in the meadow he saw his sister on the path. The tiny girl was trudging along, falling down then getting up. She kept moving farther and farther away from the safety of the camp and the elders. He was afraid she was following him.

Surely, she would turn back. He was very annoyed with her. Why did she always want to follow him? He didn't want to have to go down and take her back to camp. He wanted to climb higher with his cousins. Cousin Flea was already high above him. The boys would get to the top without him.

Dog Cry turned and saw his cousins were far above him. Flea was jumping around. "Come on!" the boys called. Always Angry waved down to him and pointed higher to show him where the cousins were going to climb next.

Chapter Five

Dog Cry turned and saw his cousins were far above him. Flea was jumping around. "Come on!" the boys called. Always Angry waved down to him and pointed higher to show him where the cousins were going to climb next.

The boys scrambled up and over the rock pile and found themselves high on a ledge overlooking the whole campground.

Far down below them, Dog Cry and his cousins could see their fathers with the men from all the Chukchansi villages. The men were building shelters, fishing, and clearing a place for the singing and dancing later that evening.

The boys could see their mothers and the women building a long cooking fire, and they could hear the laughing of the women in the camp. He could see the elders sitting in the shade of the shelter.

"Come on," the boys shouted.

Breaks Shells coming closer to the berry bushes. She was not turning back. Her tiny feet were moving her closer to the bottom of the hill. Her hair swung as she moved along. He didn't know what to do.

As he watched her, he saw a long, strange shadow in the gully at the bottom of the hill.

The shadow wasn't the color of the berry bushes shadows. Instead it was a dull tan color. Then the strange shadow moved, but there was no wind.

Dog Cry couldn't believe what he saw. Crouched in the cover of the berry bushes at the edge of the gully was a great, tawny mountain lion, bigger than a man. And Breaks Shells was stop-starting, falling and getting up again. She was moving in her steady way, closer and closer to the lion.

One of his cousins called to him. The boys were laughing again as they raced each other in climbing up the ledge to get to the top of the hill.

The oldest of his cousins was a boy who was called Always Angry. He seldom spoke and almost never smiled. Always Angry grabbed a knotty little tree and pulled himself up and climbed until he was two man lengths above the other boys.

Dog Cry wanted to climb with his cousins, but he was worried. He didn't see his sister with the elders. He didn't know where she was.

He could see where the women of the four villages were preparing food. He could see his mother lift her cooking basket and go toward the fire line. Little Breaks Shells was not with her. He looked at the elders as they sat talking. He still could not see his sister.

Looking down at the camp, he could see the narrow path where he had run to meet his cousins. It ran from the campground across the meadow to the bottom of the hill. He saw the dry meadow grass all yellow in the sun.

Far from the elders, far from the campground, and deep in the meadow he saw his sister on the path.

The little girl was trudging along, moving farther and farther away from the safety of the camp as she was following him.

Her black hair shone against the dry yellow grasses as she came closer to the berry bushes at the bottom of the hill.

He was very annoyed with her. Why did she always want to follow him? He didn't want to have to go down and take her back to camp. He wanted to climb higher with his cousins. Cousin Flea was already high above him. The boys would get to the top without him.

Dog Cry turned and saw his cousins were far above him. Flea was jumping around. "Come on!" the boys called. Always Angry waved down to him and pointed higher to show him where the cousins were going to climb next.

Dog Cry looked down and saw Breaks Shells coming closer to the berry bushes. She was not turning back. Her tiny feet were moving her closer to the bottom of the hill. Her hair swung as she moved along. He didn't know what to do.

As he watched her, he saw a long, strange shadow in the gully at the bottom of the hill.

The shadow wasn't the color of the berry bushes shadows. Instead it was a dull tan color. Then the strange shadow moved, but there was no wind. Dog Cry couldn't believe what he saw. Crouched in the cover of the berry bushes at the edge of the gully was a great, tawny mountain lion, bigger than a man.

Breaks Shells was moving in her steady way closer and closer to the lion.

Chapter Six

Dog Cry didn't know what to do. Worried thoughts came swirling through his mind and filled it up.

Lions had more power than Nasis. The spirit of a lion was cunning and bold. His grandfather had told him that only a grizzly bear had a strong enough spirit to challenge a lion. Dog Cry just stared down at his sister and the great cat waiting for her.

On the other side of the berry bushes, Breaks Shells took two more steps along the path. She was moving toward the lion.

Dog Cry's mind settled and he knew what he had to do. He began to run down the hill as fast as he could run. He was running to his sister. Going faster and faster, he though he might trip when he came to the rock fall. But he could not stop. If he could make himself a target, the lion might ignore Breaks Shells.

He ran down so fast it felt ike he was flying. His feet barely touched the hard surface of the steep slopping rock pile.

He didn't worry about Nassis. He didn't even worry about the claws or teeth of the lion. He only worried about his little sister, and running down the hill as fast as his legs could run.

Dog Cry's toes skidded in the dirt beyond the rocks. He started to slide in the soft dust and leaves, but caught himself and continued racing downhill. He was swift and fleet.

His own spirit called to the spirits of elk and deer to help him, for they ran light and very fast, but he knew that elk and deer never ran toward danger. He did not think that they would help him run to danger.

He prayed that although elk and deer did not have courage, they woud give him their speed. His spirit called to theirs anyway. Elk and deer did help him. His feet were fleet and he didn't trip on the rocks as he ran.

Suddenly he found himself at the bottom of the hill and on the edge of the gully. He came to a stop just across from the great tan beast, and he saw its yellow eyes and long white fangs. He saw its sharp claws.

Breaks Shells came around the berry bushes and saw her brother and the ion.

The mountain lion shook his smooth head and his ears grew flatter. His eyes narrowed and he snarled at the little girl.

Lion looked across the gully at Dog Cry and snarled at the boy for interferring. He looked from Dog Cry to Breaks Shells and back again. The lion began to inch toward the little girl.

Dog Cry screamed again and again. He put both his arms up in the air as high as he could reach. The lion turned his head toward the boy.

Dog Cry didn't have time to be afraid. A feeling came into his throat and he began to make up a song. Instead of screaming, he sang, "Ta ne, ta ne we he sit." He sang as loudly as he could. "Ta ne, ta ne we he sit."

As he jumped into the gully, the boy grabbed at a broken berry vine. He didn't even notice that its stickers punctured his hand. He waved the vine at the lion with one hand and waved his snake stick with the other.

He moved toward the lion singing his song. More song words came to him and he sang louder, *"Hi ama wok ye. Hi ama wok ye la pa he. Ta ne, ta ne we he sit."*

He knew the lion was bigger than his father and his claws were sharper than spears or arrowheads. He knew the lion could kill him as easily as it killed a deer or coyote.

~≪◇≫~

Chapter Seven

Dog Cry danced in front of the lion, waving the vine. He sang his best song, as loudly as he could.

The cousins on the hillside behind him came sliding and tumbling down. Cousin Flea was yelling, and the cousins were all shouting so loudly that the birds had all left the oak trees and the bushes and had flown to the meadow.

All the people from the camp began to run across the meadow to see what the commotion by the berry bushes was all about.

The big lion watched the boy switching the air and moving toward him. The lion heard the Chukchansi song coming from the boy's mouth. Dog Cry's cousins heard his song too, and they joined in his singing. *"Hi ama wok ye la pa he. Ta ne, ta ne we he sit,"* the cousins sang.

The cousins grew bolder. They jumped across the gully and clustered behind Dog Cry. They waved their sticks and broken branches.

They threw small rocks and chunks of dirt at the lion. The boys jumped up and down and made fierce faces. They shrieked and yelled and sang, *"Ta ne, ta ne we he sit."*

Lion did not like Dog Cry's singing. He did not like the cousins' singing either. His powerful claws and sharp fangs could rip into all the children, but the singing hurt his ears.

Lion flattened his ears back as low on his head as he could so he wouldn't hear Dog Cry's song. Slowly, the great cat began to retreat from the noise. With his shoulders still crouched and his tail twitching, the lion moved backward, away from Dog Cry and the boys and away from Breaks Shells. He disappeared into the shrubbery by the river.

Breaks Shells was safe. The boys were safe. Dog Cry thanked the spirits of elk and deer that had helped him run down the hillside. He thanked the spirits of the ancestors of the Chukchansi who had given him courage and his song. He thanked the spirit of the lion for going away.

Breaks Shells had tears on her face as she looked past the berry bushes to her brother and cousins by the gully.

Cousin Flea began to laugh. "You are a hero, Dog Cry," he said. All the boys began to laugh. They didn't know why they were laughing.

Breaks Shells didn't know why her brother and her cousins were laughing either, but the laughing made her tears come faster. Her face was dusty and her fat cheeks had wet tracks down them. Dog Cry picked her up and held her. She was alive. She was safe.

~~~~~~

Chapter Eight

The people of the four villages had all come running down the path. They reached the berry bushes and saw the children. Men and women came. Teenagers came. All the girls and boys of the four villages came. Even the elders came down to the berry bushes to see what was going on. But of course, the elders came slowly.

When she pushed through the crowd, Dog Cry's mother took Breaks Shells into her arms. She asked Dog Cry what had happened. But everyone was talking all at once. The air around the berry bushes had never been so full of questions. Dog Cry couldn't talk. He couldn't answer his mother.

All the cousins began to answer all at once, each wanting to and tell what happened. Cousin Flea's squeaky voice was the loudest and he talked the most.

Flea told how his cousin from the village of Kataniu, his cousin who was named Dog Cry, had saved little Breaks Shells by chasing a huge mountain lion away.

But no one believed Cousin Flea. The other cousins tried to tell the story but the people from the four villages just shook their heads. They looked away from the boys.

"There was no lion," someone said.

Flea's father said, "No lion would come so close to camp." The people all nodded their heads.

The most elder of the elders of Tsuloniu, the largest village of the Chukchansi frowned. He wanted to know why a little girl had wandered so far from camp. "Who was watching this little granddaughter?" he asked, scowling at the boys.

One bad tempered man Dog Cry knew from the village of Kitaniu said, "You boys scared a bob cat, not a lion. You disturbed camp for nothing."

No one wanted to believe the boys that a lion had come so close to camp.

Always Angry, the oldest of the cousins, stepped forward. In front of the headman of Apasau he said, "My cousin from the village of Kataniu fought a lion, not a bob cat. We know what bob cats look like and what lions look like.

Always Angry, who seldom talked, turned to look straight at all the men and the elders.

"This was a lion," he said slowly and clearly. "A great tan lion. It was fierce. It was as big as a man and it had fangs as long as a man's hand. It was lying in the gully here behind the berries.

"It would have killed her. Maybe it would have killed all of us. Dog Cry fought it with only a berry vine and a stick in his hands."

The headman of Apasau, host of the summer camp, frowned and stepped down into the shalow gully. The people of the four villages of the Chukchansi watched as he carefully examined the ground in the shade of the berry bushes. Then he turned to the people. He held his hand up so everyone would be quiet.

"People," he said, "the boy, Always Angry, is my son. I know him well. He does not speak unless he has something to say. He is truthful.

The headman went on talking. "He told us that Dog Cry frightened a lion. We don't want to believe that a lion came so close to camp. But this was not a bobcat. This was a lion, a very large lion." He pointed to the soft dirt at the edge of the gully closest to the berry bushes.

"Look," he said. "It's tracks are here in the dust."

The headman held up his left hand and spread the fingers wide apart. Everyone was quiet.

The headman of Apasau, smiled at the boys. "A bobcat does not have feet bigger than a man's hand," he said.

"A bobcat's body is not longer than a man's body." He looked at the people with a serious face.

"What these boys say is the truth. The boy from Kataniu called Dog Cry is a boy not yet big enough to go on a hunt or even into a sweat lodge with men. But he drove a lion away with a berry vine."

〰〰〰〰〰〰〰〰〰〰〰〰〰〰〰〰〰〰〰〰〰〰〰〰

CHAPTER NINE

Cousin Flea couldn't be completely still while the headman of Apasau, the host of the whole summer camp, was speaking. Cousin Flea interrupted to squeak, " Dog Cry didn't scare the lion away with a berry vine. He scared the lion away with his singing!"

This, of course, made all the people laugh. The headman and the most elder of all the elders laughed too.

Dog Cry's mother held Breaks Shells up for everyone to see. She looked at her daughter nd her son and smiled.

Dog Cry looked at her and he knew she was happy with him. His father stood in the crowd and he too looked at his son. Dog Cry knew his father was proud of him on this day.

The headman of Apasau, host of the summer campout for four villages, held up both hands and the crowd quieted down.

He straightened up and waited until even the babies and little children became quiet and the elders had stopped grumbling. Then, the headman of Apasau looked over at the old man who was the most elder of the elders of Tsuloniu, the largest village of the Chukchansi, and they solemnly nodded to each other.

The most elder of the elders of Tsuloniu, the largest village of the Chukchansi, spoke to Dog Cry. "From this day," you will be known by a new name. It is Lion Singer."

The old man nodded at Dog Cry, and he smiled at the boy who was once Dog Cry. "A boy by the name of Lion Singer has brought honor to all the villages of the Chukchansi tribe on this day," the old man said in a rough, strong voice. "His story belongs to all of our villages."

~~~~~~~~~~~~~~~~~~~~~~~~~~~~~~~~~~~~~~~

CHAPTER TEN

The headman of Apasau, host of the summer campout for four villages, held up both hands and the crowd quieted down. He straightened up and waited until even the babies and little children became quiet and the elders had stopped grumbling.

Then, the headman of Apasau looked over at the old man who was the most elder of the elders of Tsuloniu, the largest village of the Chukchansi, and they solemnly nodded to each other.

The most elder of the elders of Tsuloniu, the largest village of the Chukchansi, spoke to Dog Cry. "From this day," you will be always be known by this name. He put his hand on Lion Singer's head, and then sang a song

The old man nodded at Dog Cry, and he smiled. "A boy by the name of Lion Singer has brought honor to all the villages of the Chukchansi tribe on this day," the old man said in a rough, strong voice. "His story belongs to all of our villages."

The people smiled as they turned to go back to the campground. Many people reached out to softly touch Lion Singer's back or arm as they passed him.

None of the Chukchansi people ever scolded Lion Singer for having left his sister and gone to play with his cousins. The people saw Lion Singer with his mother and sister, and they knew he had already learned that serious lesson well enough.

The Chukchansi men and women were very wise. They did not waste time saying what didn't need to be said.

As they walked back to the campground, Lion Singer began to have proud thoughts. He even had the thought that one of the storytellers might make a story-song about him in the camp that night. But, while the boy called Lion Singer was having proud thoughts, the boy who was once called Dog Cry was thinking serious thoughts. He was very glad he had cousins. They had bravely helped him fight a lion. He knew he had needed their help, and that they came to help when he needed them.

Lion Singer thought that cousins were nearly the best thing in his life. He *knew* that his little sister, Breaks Shells, was the very, very best thing in his life.

<<<<> <>>>>

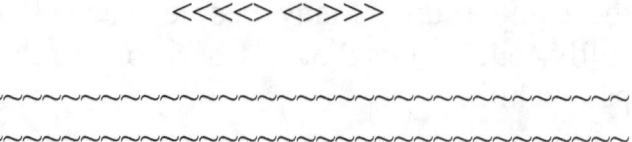

Note on Lion Singer's song:

We he sit = 'mountain lion.'
Ta ne = 'go away.'
Hi ama wok ye la pa he = "this one gives the whip."

****

THINGS TO KNOW
ABOUT BLUE JAY GIRL AND LION
SINGER'S TRIBAL HISTORY

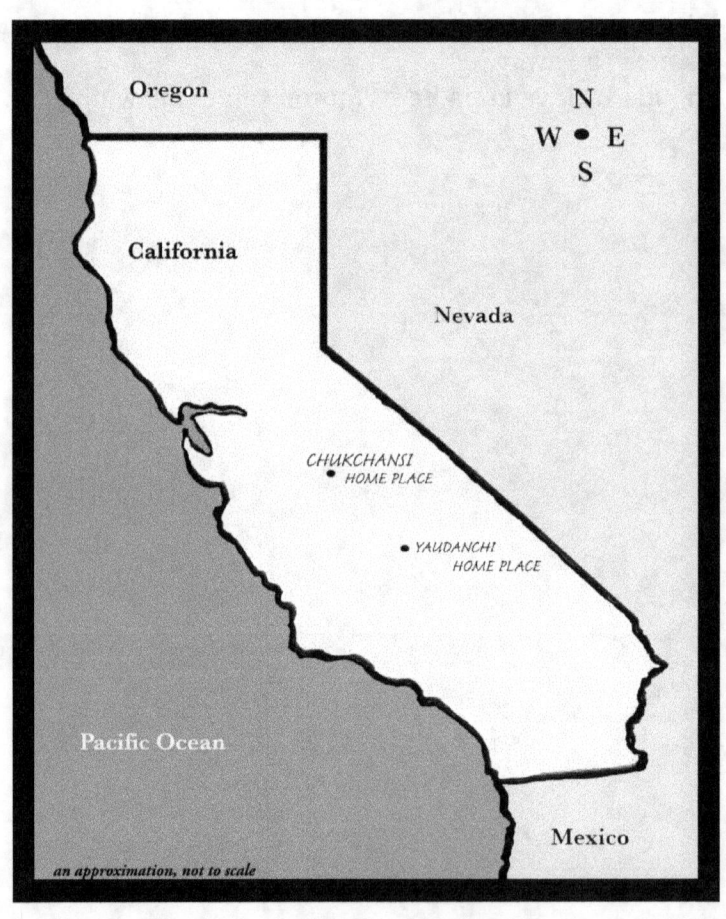

The place where Blue Jay Girl and Lion Singer lived a long time ago, is called California nowdays. It is one of the fifty states of the United States of America. California is bordered by by the Pacific Ocean on the west; by other states, Oregon to the north, Nevada and Arizona to the east; and by Mexico on the south.

Until the 1500s, the people of North and South America were separate from the people of Asia, Europe and Africa. At that time, California had no special name or boundaries. It was just a place of open land.

Its hills and valleys were populated by many small tribes of Native People. The land was wooded with oak and other deciduous trees in the valleys and foothills, and tall conifers in the high mountains. It had streams and rivers coming down from the mountains.

In those old days, before California had boundaries and was mapped as one of the United States, the Native People lived in villages throughout the large area that became the state. Some Native People lived in valleys, some in the mountains, some along the coast.

The tribes had different languages, but traded with each other in historically peaceful ways in the area of California where the Yokuts people lived. The Yokuts tribes' languages were similar to each other.

The Yokuts lived on the west side of the mountains now called the Sierra Nevada of California. Blue Jay Girl and Lion belonged to the group of tribes called the Yokuts. Lion Singer's tribe was the farthest north of any of the Yokuts group. Blue Jay Girl's tribe was farther south, and there were other tribes of Yokuts between them.

Today the descendants of Lion Singer's Chukchansi tribe still maintain a rancheria in the area the tribe had lived far back into time. It is near the present-day town of Oakhurst.

The descendants of Blue Jay Girl's Yaudanchi tribe, along with other Yokuts tribes who were gathered together years ago by the government, share a large reservation near the towns of Porterville, Springville, and Terra Bella.

Perhaps more than a thousand years ago, the Yokuts group of tribes had settled in the long stretch of hill country of what is now eastern Madera, Fresno, Kings, Tulare, and Kern Counties of California.

The foothills of the Sierra were rich in the things people needed to have good lives. With plentiful game, hunting was easy. Squirrel, rabbit, possum, porcupine, deer, elk, and both brown and grizzly bears provided ample meat, and also the leather and furs needed to make comfortable clothing and household items.

The large stands of many varieties of oak and other deciduous trees provided acorns thaat were harvested in the fall, carefully stored and made into meal as needed.

Nature also provided edible insects, birds, and fish. Many kinds of native berries, nuts and fruits were used to flavor and preserve food. They traded with each other, and with the tribes on their borders, such as the Miwok tribe on the north, and the Monache on the east.

Trading among all the Native Peoples was common. Even with tribes who had languages different from the Yokuts. The people could get salt and dried ocean fish from the people along the Pacific Coast, and obsidian for arrow heads from the people across the high Sierra. Historians believe that there were few wars among the Native People's tribes in what is now California, and that there was usually peace among them for thousands of years.

*

Acknowledgements

The stories of *Blue Jay Girl* and *Lion Singer* would never have been published without encouragement and help from Kathleen Simpson, Margaret Dubin, Malcolm Margolin, and the Tule River Indian Reservation. The first edition of each of the books were featured in National Parks and Indian Museums across the nation.

Here is the story of how the books came about. Early in 2004, Kathleen Simpson, then the tribal administrator for the Picayune Rancheria of Chukchansi Indians, asked me if I would do something for the education program of the tribe. My writing had been featured in an award-winning quarterly and had been included in some anthologies. I, and other artists and poets, had given readings around the state as part of a two year long exhibit: *Sing Me Your Story, Dance Me Home*. Kathleen asked me for a story that might help the the boys in the program take pride in their heritage. I agreed, and began writing LION SINGER.

However, before the book was quite finished, the Picayune Council changed its direction, Kathleen was replaced as its administrator, and the children's project was dropped. I was left with a manuscript and drawings that had no place to go. I sent them to my editor at Heyday Books in Berkeley. Margaret Dubin was my editon there. Although at that time, the company didn't publish children's books, Heyday's publisher, Malcolm Margolin, read the manuscript and liked it. What the Picayune rejected, Heyday Books accepted.

Lion Singer, was joined by the next Yokuts-based book I wrote, *Blue Jay Girl*. Eventually the two books found a place for themselves in Indian venues all around the nation. First of all, I thank Kathleen Simpson, Malcolm Margolin, and his editor Margaret Dubin who gave him the raw manuscript, and also thank a man named Mane Hunter, of the Tule River Indian Reservation, who once a long time ago gave me the inspiration for the story of *Lion Singer*.

A few years later, I began to write its companion book *Blue Jay Girl*. Since I had been fortunate enough to have been a teacher for twenty years,at the school that the children from the Tule Indian Reservation, I decided to feature one of the tribes of the Tule in this book.

The Tule River Indian Reservation is is a very large reservation with members from a number of Yokuts tribes: Wakchumi, Choinumni, Yaudanchi, and others. These tribes had been scattered by the American settlers in the late 19th century over an area that now encompasses three or four large counties of California. During the early twentieth century, these scattered people were gathered up by army soldiers and marched on foot to a central location east of the town of Porterville. Then later, as American farmers coveted the arable land of the reservation, the people were moved again fourteen miles farther east into the hills. It is a sad story, but today in the twenty-first century, the 'Rez' is a thriving place.

I chose to concentrate the story I wrote on a child from the Yaudanchi tribe, the tribe who long ago lived in the physical space of the land that became the reservation.

Thank you, Kathleen, Margaret, Malcolm. And, thanks to a very generous grant from the Tule Indian Reservations Tribal Council, *Blue Jay Girl* followed *Lion Singer* into publication by Heyday Books. The Rez has my forever gratitude.

Sylvia Ross February 6, 2019

Apologia

For teachers who might use this book in their classrooms, please know that I realize that these two stories are out-of-sync with the socio-cultural climate of today. Alas, the female protagonist of *Blue Jay Girl* does not grow up to be a fierce warrior.

In one of *Lion Singer's* early reviews, a librarian dismissed the story as "…just another book where the hero is a boy." I knew as I began writing *Blue Jay Girl*, that the end of this story wouldn't meet that librarian's requirements either. It doesn't suit the cultural ethos of today. The protagonist, Blue Jay Girl, does not become a captain of either industry or war. She becomes a healer, following a traditional role for women throughout time. But I made that choice. Mea culpa, mea culpa, mea maxima culpa.

However, I make no apology for the *gender* of the hero of LION SINGER. An event I'd witnessed years before, inspired the story of LION SINGER. I was teaching third grade at a school where many pupils came daily by bus from the Tule River Indian Reservation, fourteen miles away. The bell had rung signaling the end of the school day. There were about three hundred children in the primary grades alone, in our semi-rural school. Nearly all of our students were bussed to and from our school daily.

Consequently, we teachers watched the yard until all the children were in the bus and on their way home. Depending on traffic, the busses that came to pick up our students were sometimes late. The wiggly young kindergarten and first graders were customarily gathered to stand first in line at the appropriate bus gate with their teachers.

The older children knew the drill and all the rules. Their teachers didn't need to line them up at the correct gate. The older students had the freedom of the playground, shooting marbles, laughing, and chatting with friends from other rooms. We second and third grade teachers on duty usually enjoyed it for we had the chance to mingle informally with the children, visiting with them, doing a different kind of teaching.

That one afternoon, a few kids from the Rez were clustered with me under a big tree, talking about something or other. Suddenly, one of my third graders, a boy named Mane Hunter, took off running. Though an artist by nature, and not particularly athletic, the boy zoomed through the crowded playground. Zigzagging through teachers and children who were in his way, he cut a diagonal across the yard, blasting headlong toward the most distant gate as the big busses began coming into the drive. I have no idea how he could have seen or known what was happening so far away. But he did.

What had happened was that a sudden gust of wind had come up whirling dust. It pulled the work papers in Mane's little sister's hands away from her. As she stood lined up with her first grade class, the papers flew up and over the fence and scattered on the bus driveway. Little sister slipped through the gate, ignoring the rules, and going into danger. She was bent down in the drive trying to retrieve her classwork papers as the busses approached. Her teacher, busy with another child's troubles, didn't see what had happened. The work papers were lost, but Mane was able to pull his sister back through the gate. She was safe.

There is often truth in fiction. Sometimes heroes *are* boys.

sr

www.ingramcontent.com/pod-product-compliance
Lightning Source LLC
Chambersburg PA
CBHW070341130626
46556CB00007B/2969